#3 Catacombs Mysteries©

The Beginning of the End

Mary Litton

To Art and Jenny

www.MaryLitton.com

Catacombs Mysteries, illustrations and text copyright

© 2012 Mary Litton

Editor: Jack Bradford
Interior Director: Elizabeth Clare
ISBN:0615745490
ISBN-13:9780615745497

CONTENTS

1

UNDERCOVER

The fallen leaves surrounding St. John's Church had dried into a crunchy brown carpet that covered the ground. A few red and yellow leaves clung to their mostly bare branches, refusing to let go of autumn.

Other leaves danced in the crisp wind around the families who walked toward the church. Kids zipped up their jackets and shoved their hands in their pockets to keep warm from the chill on their way to Sunday services.

Inside the church, Will sat with his family in one of the middle pews. He looked okay in his blue button-down shirt and his only pair of khaki pants, but his mismatched socks were a dead giveaway that, like every Sunday morning, he had rushed to get to church on time. He tried to pull his pant legs down so that his one brown sock and one blue sock didn't show.

He watched the other families fill the seats in the pews around him. Usually, as he waited for service to begin, he liked to doodle in a small notebook that his mom kept in her pocketbook. But this morning, he used it to take notes.

He was on the lookout for strange behavior. He and his friend Molly had to find out who kept getting into the basement's time portal and changing the Bible stories. So far, two Bible stories had been changed, but Molly and Will had been able to go back through the portal and fix them before anything bad

had happened. Angie, the angel God sent
to help them, had asked them to do some
detective work to find out who was
sneaking down there and causing these
changes.

After the service started, Will and the
other kids went to the Fellowship Hall
for the kids' lesson. He walked in to find
a seat on the floor with the rest of his
third-grade class, but nearly tripped
when he noticed Molly.

Instead of sitting with the other
second-graders, she was standing in the
back of the room. She wore a purple
dress with neon green leggings, a large
floppy straw hat, and oversized black
sunglasses. She was concentrating on
writing in a small notebook.

Will walked over to her. "Molly?" he
asked.

When Molly looked up at him, she
shook her head and put her finger to her
lips, as if telling him to be quiet.

"What are you doing?" Will asked.

"I'm undercover," Molly whispered.
"I'm watching and taking notes on all
suspicious activity."

"The only suspicious thing I see is
what you're wearing," Will said.

"We have to figure out who is getting into the time portal," Molly replied, glaring at him over the rim of the large glasses. "The only way we can do that is to watch who goes into the basement. I've been taking notes all morning."

"My dears, have a seat," called Mrs. Smotherly, the children's lesson leader. She clapped her hands to get the group's attention as she waddled up to the front of the room. Her white hair formed a perfect cloud-like circle around her head, and she had just applied a fresh coat of sticky orange lipstick. She peered at the class through her large, thick-rimmed glasses. "One, two, three, eyes on me," she called, receiving a weak response of "One, two, eyes on you," from only a few kids.

Will looked through the door to the kitchen, where the church grandmothers were preparing coffee and snacks for after the service. A brown curly ponytail stood out among the heads of white and grey. Suddenly, the woman with the ponytail turned around and winked at

Will.

Will was surprised when he recognized Angie, the angel who helped them in their last two missions.

"Molly," Will nudged her. "In the kitchen—it's Angie!"

Molly looked up but didn't see her. Will looked again and realized she was gone. Suddenly, the cross in his pocket began to get warm, and he knew they were being called to the time portal. "She was just here, and now my cross is getting warm," Will said. "We have to get to the catacombs."

2

OLD YELLER

"William!" Mrs. Smotherly called across the room. Will looked up. Everyone was staring at him. His stomach flip-flopped and his cheeks grew warm in embarrassment. He hated to get in trouble.

"Would you like to share what is so important that you feel the need to interrupt my lesson?"

"Um, no," Will grumbled, looking down at the floor.

"Well, then, come on up here and take a seat with your class," Mrs. Smotherly pointed toward a spot on the floor in front of her. All the kids looked at Will. He knew he had to go see Angie because she only appeared when there was trouble, but he did not want to break the rules.

Mrs. Smotherly waited, and everyone sat quietly, waiting for Will.

Will's stomach tied up in knots, and his face felt like it was on fire. As his mind raced to think of a way to get out of class, Molly took a step forward.

"Will can't join the class right now," she said firmly.

Mrs. Smotherly raised an eyebrow and said, "Why not, Molly?"

"He was just saying that he had to go to the bathroom," Molly announced to the whole room. A few kids snickered. Molly grinned and added, "He said it's so bad that he's about to burst like Old Yeller!"

Mrs. Smotherly's mouth dropped

open, and the children erupted into laughter. Molly tugged Will by the elbow as she headed toward the door. "And I have to go, too!"

"Children! Quiet!" Mrs. Smotherly called over the laughter as Molly pulled Will out the door. "Manners!" she snapped just as the door shut behind them.

Will could feel Mrs. Smotherly's glare through the door. "I can't believe you just said that," Will said, his face still burning with embarrassment.

"I know!" Molly grinned, very pleased with herself.

"And Old Yeller is a dog. That made no sense."

"I thought Old Yeller was that geyser that shoots water into the air like a volcano."

"That's Old *Faithful*. It's in Yellowstone National Park."

"Thanks for the geography lesson,"

Molly said sarcastically, shaking her head. "You *could* just say thank you for my help." Suddenly Molly felt self-conscious for being wrong in front of the whole class. Why did she have to say something dumb?

Seeing that he hurt her feelings, Will felt bad for correcting Molly. "Sorry, Molly," he muttered. "I didn't mean to hurt your feelings."

"It's okay." Molly shrugged. "I just don't like being told when I get things wrong."

"Well, one thing you didn't get wrong," Will said with a grin, "was getting us out of class."

Molly smiled. "It's my specialty!"

"My cross is getting warmer," Will said, remembering why they left.

"So is mine," Molly replied, feeling the cross she wore around her neck. "That must mean someone has broken in and changed another Bible story."

"Yeah," Will agreed, turning toward the stairs that led to the basement. "We better hurry downstairs and find Angie!"

3

THE LIST OF SUSPECTS

Will started running down the stairs, but noticed that Molly was taking them very slowly. "Hurry up!" Will called.

"I can't see anything through these glasses," Molly said. She stretched out her arms to feel around in front of her as if she were blindfolded. "They're too dark!"

"Then take them off," Will said. "What good are spy glasses if you can't see through them?"

Molly pulled them off and smiled. "That's so much better!"

"What about the hat?" Will asked.

Molly glanced up at the brim above her forehead. She had to admit it was getting a bit itchy. She took it off and tucked her glasses inside it, hiding them in a corner by the stairs. "Much better," she said, shaking out her long blonde hair.

"I put a flashlight on a chain with my cross so that we'll always have it," Will said, pulling it out of his pocket to show her.

"Cool," said Molly. "It's like a charm necklace!"

"It is *not* a charm necklace," he said, taking offense. "Girls wear charm necklaces."

"Fine," Molly said, rolling her eyes. "It's like the janitor's key ring. Is that better?"

Will smiled. "Yes. It's like Mr. Habersham's key chain."

"He's one of the suspects I listed in my notebook this morning," Molly said. "Mr. Habersham has keys to all of these rooms, and he can walk through the hallways without anyone noticing."

"But that's his job," Will said. Mr. Habersham was a tall, skinny bald man with a constant sneer on his face. He was never friendly, and in fact, he always seemed a little scary. But Will and the other boys thought he was cool because he could go anywhere and get into all sorts of locked rooms.

Molly ignored his comment and added, "There's also a lurker who sits in the back during service. I've seen her before. She comes in late and sits in the last pew, and as soon as service is over, she runs out without talking to anyone."

Will had also seen this tiny woman. She had short brown hair and glasses, and she always seemed really nervous. She reminded him of a mouse, skittering around, trying not to be seen.

When they reached the bottom floor, Will turned on his flashlight and they started down the hallway that they called the catacombs. Will's flashlight was small and only provided a little light, so they had to strain their eyes to see ahead. They no longer needed the map, but they still went slowly so they wouldn't make a wrong turn in the dark.

A faint sound in the distance stopped Will dead in his tracks. Molly ran right into him, nearly knocking him over.

"Hey," Molly started to complain, but Will shushed her.

"Did you hear that?" Will whispered.

Molly stood perfectly still, listening. The catacombs should be empty, everyone else was upstairs in service.

Everyone except the person changing the Bible stories.

Fear gripped Molly as she hoped Will was wrong. She was not ready to confront their suspect in a dark hallway where no one could hear them scream. The only sound she heard was her heartbeat, pounding in her chest.

Suddenly she heard a faint sound. It was coming from behind them.

They held their breath and strained to hear more clearly. It was the sound of footsteps.

4

CAUGHT IN THE ACT

Will and Molly instantly knew they were not alone in the catacombs. Someone was behind them and catching up fast. They both jumped, and Molly covered her mouth with her hand to keep from screaming.

"Let's go!" Will whispered. He grabbed Molly's hand and started to run. He took a sharp left so quickly that Molly had to grab the back of his shirt to keep up with him.

The footsteps got louder and faster. Someone was chasing them!

Will turned down the final hallway and skidded to a stop. "The door is here somewhere," he said, panting. They looked for the small handle that led them into room 3C, but the beam from Will's flashlight was not strong enough.

The footsteps were getting even closer. Will flashed his light all around the wall, his hands sweating. He looked over his shoulder but could not see anything in the darkness.

Suddenly, they both saw the faint light of another flashlight. Molly inhaled sharply and dropped Will's hand. She ran along the length of the wall, feeling with both hands until finally she touched something hard and cold sticking out of the wall.

"Here!" she called, grabbing Will and pushing open the door just as the other flashlight beam rounded the corner.

They fell through the door and into the dark room, rushing toward the far corner just as they heard the doorknob turn behind them. The door opened, and a ray of light swept across both sides of the room. Will and Molly held their breath and pressed up against the wall, hoping to avoid the beam of light.

The person walked to the middle of the room and grabbed the chain attached to the light bulb.

They were cornered. As they gripped each other's hands in terror, they realized they were in the same room with the person who had been changing the Bible stories. They were finally about to see who was trying to change Christianity.

They crouched down behind a box and held their breath.

CLICK!

The room filled with light.

Molly closed her eyes. Will jumped. And Mr. Habersham yelled sharply, in surprise.

"What are you kids doing in here?" Mr. Habersham demanded. "You scared me!"

Molly crouched into her best karate pose, with one hand out in front of her like a knife blade. "Why are you chasing us?" she demanded, narrowing her eyes.

Will balled his hands into fists and put them in the air, ready for a fight. He hoped Mr. Habersham couldn't see how much they were shaking.

"I'm not chasing anyone," Mr. Habersham snapped. "I'm the only one who is supposed to be down here. What are you two doing, sneaking around down here?" he demanded, pointing a long, bony finger at them.

"Father Dan gave us a map to the room," Will said.

"Kids have no place running around down here in the basement," Mr. Habersham mumbled. He was standing right under the pull chain that led to the time portal.

Mr. Habersham reached up for the light. Molly gasped and lunged forward. "What do you think you're doing?" she demanded, grabbing the chain from his reach. Will rushed over with his fists in the air, ready to protect Molly.

Mr. Habersham stared at them as if

they were crazy. "I'm changing the light bulb!" he growled, pulling a fresh bulb out of his pocket. Will and Molly looked up and saw that the bulb was flickering.

"Oh," Molly said, backing away, her hands falling to her sides.

Will's legs suddenly turned to jelly as he tried to back away. His heart pounded as he dropped his fists.

"You scared us!" Molly said. "We thought you were stealing something."

"And I suppose you two kids are church security?" Mr. Habersham grumbled as he screwed in a new bulb.

"Yes, we are," Will answered confidently.

Mr. Habersham shook his head and gave them a look that could melt a popsicle. "I don't know what Father Dan put you kids up to, but I don't want to ever catch you down here in this basement again."

Without another word, Mr.

Habersham shook his head and left the room. His footsteps echoed down the hallway until silence finally surrounded Molly and Will.

Will sighed heavily with relief.

"I thought we were going to have to fight him," Molly said, shaking her head. Then something caught her eye. She looked over and screamed as she saw someone standing in the corner of the room.

"It's just me," Angie said in a soothing voice, holding out her hands in a peaceful gesture.

"Would everyone please stop scaring me?" Molly cried, putting her hand in front of her pounding heart.

"Wow," Angie said. "You two sure are jumpy today."

"You'd be jumpy too if you had to sneak around pitch-dark catacombs looking for a secret time portal," Molly panted.

"Of course I would," Angie agreed. "You handled Mr. Habersham well. You're getting good at this. Nice disguise upstairs, Molly. I hardly recognized you."

Molly smiled proudly. "Thanks. I had to go undercover to make notes on suspicious people. We have to figure out who's getting in here."

"Do you have any leads?"

"Mr. Habersham was one suspect," Will said. "He does have keys and comes down here a lot."

Angie thought a moment and said, "Whoever is breaking into the time portal was already here this morning. The person changed another Bible story, so we need your help to get in there and correct it before it changes all of Christianity." Angie frowned and tapped her earpiece as she looked up at the ceiling.

Will shook his head. He couldn't get used to talking to an angel that used a cell phone to talk to God.

"They're here and ready to go," she said into the air. She listened for another second and then looked back at them. "He's glad to see you and said you were both really brave just then. He says that this is a tough one, but remember: He's right there with you."

Will and Molly looked at each other. They were scared, but they nodded. They knew that with God's help, they could be brave.

They walked over to the chain hanging from the brand-new light bulb.

"The verse that will take you back in time is Romans 8:9, NIV. 'Nothing can separate us from God's love.'"

"Wow," Molly whispered. "Where do you suppose we're going?" she asked Will.

Will shook his head. He was nervous, and his stomach began to turn like it did on the first day of school. For some reason, he felt like this was going to be bigger than their last adventure.

Angie's normally calm eyes filled with concern as she looked at Will and Molly. "Just remember to be strong. You are never alone."

"On the count of three?" Will asked in a shaky voice. He held his cross in one hand and gripped the chain in the other. Molly gulped as she held her cross in a sweaty hand. She hesitated for a minute, looking to Angie for comfort. Angie smiled at her and said, "Have faith."

Molly nodded as she extended her other hand to grab the chain. "Nothing can separate us from God's love!" they repeated, and pulled the chain.

5

PARADISE

As soon as the chain clicked, a strong wind blew through Will and Molly's hair and clothes, and suddenly a bright spotlight filled the room. It was so bright, they had to cover their eyes and bury their faces in their arms. Will tightened his grip on the chain as he felt his feet leave the ground. Molly's stomach began to drop as she felt herself twisting and twirling through time.

Suddenly everything went dark and still. Molly slowly opened her eyes and blinked twice. She could not believe what she saw.

Will squinted and rubbed his eyes. His mouth dropped open as he turned around in a circle, looking at everything around him.

It was beautiful.

It was paradise.

They were standing on a grassy hill dotted with cattle quietly chewing grass and gently mooing. Below them, a light breeze blew through thick trees and bushes full of colorful fruits and blooms. It was like someone had cut out pictures of all of Molly's favorite plants and flowers and planted them in real life.

"It's like we're in the prettiest garden in the world," Molly whispered.

Birds swooped gracefully overhead, singing pretty melodies, and animals roamed peacefully in the distance. A river of sparkling clear water ran beside the hill and cut a path through the middle of the garden. The water looked so clean and refreshing that it made Will thirsty.

Suddenly Molly gasped and her hands flew up to cover her mouth. She turned bright red and a nervous giggle escaped from her lips.

"What is it?" Will asked, looking around. Way off in the distance, he saw a man and a woman picking fruit off a row of bushes.

They were naked.

Will blushed deep red and could not help but stare as the man and woman just stood out in the open, without any clothes on at all. He tried very hard not to laugh, but he was so embarrassed, a small chuckle spilled out of his mouth.

The two people stopped and turned to look.

Will and Molly quickly ran to a clump of trees with large pink blooms. They hid behind the trunks and burst into a fit of laughter.

After a few minutes, Molly was finally able to speak. "Don't they realize they're naked?" she asked, wiping the tears from her eyes. She tried really hard to stop giggling, but she was so embarrassed for them.

"We must be in the Garden of Eden," Will said, leaning back into the full, soft grass. He was exhausted from laughing so hard.

Molly agreed. "Then they must be Adam and Eve. We got here before they could eat the fruit from the Tree of Knowledge. They don't know they should cover up with clothes until after they eat the fruit."

She giggled again and leaned back on the grass, looking out over paradise. "What could have changed?" she asked Will.

"Let's go back through the story," Will suggested. "In the beginning, God created the heavens and earth. Then he separated light from dark to make day and night. Then he separated air from water."

"After that, he made land and covered it with all sorts of trees and plants with fruits and vegetables," Molly added.

"Then he made the sun and the moon and the stars."

"Then he made animals," Molly remembered. "First the fish in the sea, then the birds in the air, and then the animals on the ground."

"Finally, he made a man and woman in his own image," Molly continued. "He told them to eat the plants and watch over the animals. There was plenty of food for everyone and everything."

"Except that they were not to eat the fruit from one tree in the middle of the garden—the Tree of Knowledge. God told them that if they ate it, they would die."

"I have never seen anything so

beautiful. Look around," Molly said, staring in wonder at the colorful flowers and the trees full of delicious, ripe fruit.

"It's like it's the perfect climate for every single plant to flower and make fruit," Will said, looking around in awe. He had planted seeds so many times, but nothing ever grew because there always seemed to be some problem—it was too hot or too cold, or he added too much water or too little. He could not believe all of these plants could bloom at once. It was, without a doubt, a perfect environment.

6

KING OF TURKEYS

"If Adam and Eve had not eaten that fruit, we could be living here." Molly said, looking around at the beautiful garden and suddenly feeling mad. "Just look at everything they gave up. Their choice gave us sin and death."

Adam and Eve made their way even farther into the berry bushes, where they could no longer be seen. Will felt relieved, because looking at them made him feel funny.

Then they heard something strange, like an animal in trouble. They looked down toward the river and saw two large dogs barking and growling at one of the trees. All of the other animals in the garden seemed to be peaceful, but these dogs were snapping and angry, almost like guard dogs.

"Why do you think those dogs are protecting that tree?" Molly asked.

Will watched the dogs jump up and snarl at the tree. He squinted to see what was making them bark.

"Look," he said, pointing to a branch up high in the tree. "It's a puppy! It's stuck in the tree."

Molly looked to see a tiny puppy cowering on a branch. "That must be the puppy's mom and dad. They're upset because their baby is in the tree. But how did the puppy get up there?"

They looked at the poor, stuck puppy. There was no way it had climbed up by itself.

Someone had to have put it up there. Suddenly, they both understood.

"Whoever is changing the Bible stories put it up there," Molly said. "But why?"

"That must be the Tree of Knowledge. If someone wanted to change the Bible story, they would have to make it so that Adam and Eve don't eat the fruit from the tree. Adam and Eve can't get past those dogs to get the fruit."

"A serpent can't get past those dogs either," Molly added. "Remember, Adam and Eve obeyed God at first, but then an evil serpent tempted Eve with the fruit, and told her if she ate it, she would know everything. He told her that God had lied to them and did not want them to have knowledge. She believed the serpent over God and ate the fruit and gave a piece to Adam."

Anger flashed through Will. "I forget that evil is always out there in different forms, waiting for a chance to make bad choices," he said.

"But you would think that with everything they had," Molly said, waving her hand around the garden, "they would have made a better choice."

They sat back down in the soft, green grass and looked out at the beautiful landscape. Soon, they saw Adam and Eve again, blissfully picking berries, unaware of what lay ahead. They both felt very sad.

Finally, Molly stood up. "We have to get the dogs away so they can get the fruit. Let's see what kind of tools God gave us this time." Molly patted her pockets and pulled out a thin net with large holes in it, similar to the one that her soccer coach used for balls.

"Oh, no," she said, looking from the net to the dogs. "I hope we aren't supposed to catch those dogs with this net."

"Good," said Will. "You finally get the scary tool," he teased.

Will stood up and dug into his pocket. He pulled out a round plastic whistle. When he blew into it, it made a funny, gobbly squawk that made Molly giggle.

"Excuse you," she said, laughing.

Will smiled and blew it again, making them both laugh. "I know what this is, it's a turkey caller! My uncle uses one when he hunts. It's supposed to sound just like a turkey to encourage other turkeys to come near."

They looked out and saw a flock of

turkeys looking in their direction.

"Oh no!" Molly cried with a grin, "Watch out, you're going to be the King of Turkeys!"

"Do you think they're going to be my army?" asked Will.

Molly shook her head. "Come on, let's go." She started walking down the hill toward the tree.

"Wait!" Will said, grabbing her by the elbow. "I just thought of something. Adam and Eve can't see us."

"Why not?"

"Think about it," said Will. "They are the first two people. They are the only two people."

Molly's eyes got big and her mouth made an "O" as she realized what Will meant. "You're right. They would be so confused if they saw us—especially because we are wearing clothes."

"Right," said Will, suddenly very thankful for his mismatched socks and other clothes.

Molly grinned. "So we have to go top-secret, undercover?"

Will rolled his eyes and groaned. "Your favorite. What do you suggest, Agent Molly?"

Molly looked down the hill and over the horizon. The tree was on the other side of the river, out of Adam and Eve's line of sight, but they would have to sneak past them to get to that part of the garden.

"We need some disguises and a distraction," Molly said. She started picking bunches of flowers. "Have you ever made a flower crown?" she asked Will.

"I am not making a flower crown,"

Will said sharply, crossing his arms in front of his chest. "Those are for girls."

"Well, today they are for God's secret agents, so start picking."

7

FLOWER POWER

Molly began collecting flowers and showing Will how to tie the stems together into a large chain. Will grumbled and started picking and tying flowers like Molly showed him. Soon, they were both covered in flowers, camouflaging their human appearance.

Will groaned. "Nobody ever hears about this!" he warned Molly.

"I should have brought my camera!"
Molly smiled. "Flower power to the
max!"

Will was not amused. He was
determined not to get caught by anyone,
especially Adam and Eve.

"How are we going to get past them?"
Molly asked after securing her flower
belt.

"Sticks," Will suggested. He picked
up a few sticks and handed one to Molly.
"We'll throw them off in the distance, and
the sound will make Adam and Eve look
in that direction. When they are looking
the other way, we can run and hide
behind that clump of bushes over there,"
he said, pointing to some bushes about
halfway to the river.

"Sounds like a plan," Molly said.
They crouched down, ready to run.

"Ready?" Will asked, aiming his stick

toward the bushes.

Molly nodded. Will threw the stick as hard as he could into the air. It came crashing down in a clump of branches, causing Adam and Eve to stop what they were doing and look around.

"Run!" Will whispered. Crouching low to the ground in their flower disguises, they ran as fast as they could. Adam must have heard them, for he looked in their direction just as Molly slid into the bushes behind Will.

Molly peeked through the leaves and sighed with relief when she saw him look away.

"Let's throw these one more time. That will distract them enough so we can get to that large tree by the river," Will said. "Look! There are stones in the river to help us step across!"

"Thank goodness," Molly said,

relieved. "I'm so tired of getting wet when we travel to Bible stories!"

Molly held out another stick. "Ready?" she asked. Will nodded, and she launched the stick into another clump of trees. When it landed, Adam and Eve looked behind them, and Molly and Will took off running for the large tree.

As they tucked in behind the tree, Adam and Eve started walking toward the sounds.

"Good, they're going away from the river," Will said as he watched them walk back into a grove of trees.

Molly started giggling again as she watched their backsides disappear.

"Be serious," Will said, trying very hard not to smile himself. But Molly couldn't hold back, and soon she doubled over laughing. Then Will snorted as he, too, couldn't stop himself from laughing any longer. His snort made Molly laugh even harder until they were both laughing, snorting and crying.

Finally, they calmed down. "Come on," Will said, wiping the tears from his eyes. "We've got to get to the tree before they come back."

He used the stones to jump across the gentle river as Molly followed close behind. They looked over at the large tree with gnarled branches and the barking dogs below.

Molly flinched as the dogs snapped and growled up at the tree. She began to have doubts about their mission. "Why didn't God give us a weapon to fight them off? How am I supposed to use this net?"

"I'm sure we'll think of something. God gave us brains for a reason."

Molly watched the angry dogs growl and snap with their sharp teeth. Fear clenched her. "What if He's wrong?"

Will turned to face Molly. "Stop doubting yourself," he said firmly. "You sound just like Eve."

Molly gasped. "You're right," she said. "It's like Satan knows that he can whisper doubt into our minds, just like he did to Eve to make her second-guess herself."

Molly sat down and picked at the blades of grass. "I always blamed Adam and Eve for doing this to us, but now I see how easy it was to trick them into sin." She threw a blade of grass in the air and watched it blow in the light breeze. "I feel like I'm always doubting myself. I even just doubted God." She buried her head in her hands. "I think I would have believed the serpent, too. I would have eaten the fruit," she sniffed.

Will sat beside her and put his arm around her. "Don't cry."

Molly continued to talk through her tears. "As soon as they ate it, they suddenly knew about evil and sin, which made them feel guilty about being naked, so they hid from God. I just doubted God myself, and now I feel really guilty. I think I would have made the same choice, Will. I feel guilty because I think I would have chosen the fruit and made God really mad. Do you remember the story? He got really mad and sent them out of the garden."

"Yes, He was mad," Will said. "But before sending them out of the garden, He gave them clothes, remember? He was mad, but He still loved them."

"That's right," sniffed Molly.

"It reminds me about this one time that I didn't listen to my dad when he told me not to throw my baseball in the house. I thought I knew better and wouldn't hit anything, so I threw it anyway, but I ended up breaking a lamp and getting glass in my hand. My dad took the glass out and put a bandage on my hand. He was really mad, but he still took care of me."

"You think God still loves me even

though I would have made the same mistake as Eve?" Molly asked.

"Remember the verse, 'Nothing can separate us from God's love.'"

Molly nodded and wiped her eyes. She looked over at the dogs. "How are we going to get them away from the tree?"

"More distraction," Will said as he held up his turkey gobbler.

8

DOUBT

"Do you think that will work?" Molly asked.

"We have to have faith," Will replied. "Let's go hide in the bushes over there, and I'll blow. When you see them coming, throw a stick in the other direction to distract them."

They ran into a cluster of bushes and hid in the middle so they could see the dogs, but the dogs could not see them.

Will brought the turkey caller up to his lips and started blowing. A loud Gobble! Gobble! warbled through the air. The dogs' ears pointed straight up. They stopped barking and stood completely still. Will blew it again, and the dogs turned toward the sound. Will blew it one more time, and the dogs took off running in his direction.

Molly held her breath as the dogs galloped their way. Before they could reach Will in the clump of bushes, Molly launched a large stick toward the river. The loud splash made the dogs suddenly change direction and follow the sound to the water. They splashed across the river and disappeared into the woods.

"Yes!" Molly said, leaping out of the bushes. "Let's go get that puppy!"

Will stayed behind in the bushes.

"Will, what's wrong?" Molly asked, reaching in to pull him out. "Are you

53

hurt?"

Will stood up and looked around at the beautiful garden. "What if we don't change this story back?" he asked.

They stood in silence for a minute, listening to the birds' melodies float through the air, echoed by the happy lowing of the cows. Molly took a deep breath. "It's not our decision to make," she said quietly. "God made us the way we are for a reason, and He sent us back here to fix this story."

"Wouldn't it be nice not to know about everything, though? Especially the really bad stuff?" Will said.

Molly snorted. "Mr. Know-It-All doesn't want to know it all anymore?"

Sure, Will loved knowing things, but looking around at the beautiful garden, he could understand how nice it would be not to know about ugliness and sin. "If I lived here, I wouldn't care about not knowing everything."

"Yeah," Molly agreed. "It would be great if the world didn't know about sin. There wouldn't be war and scary stranger danger."

"Exactly," Will said excitedly, hoping Molly might agree with him. "If we let the story stay this way, we won't ever have to struggle with the choice of good and evil again."

"But the choice was always here," Molly said. "Adam and Eve were faced with this choice every day. Those guard dogs can't watch that tree forever. At some point, they will have to make their own choice."

"Why did God even give us the choice?" Will pouted. He kicked at the grass with the heel of his shoe.

"He gave us a brain, so He had to give

us the power of choice," Molly said. "Evil is already here. God had to let us figure out on our own to trust and believe in Him. Otherwise, He'd just control us like puppets. Then we wouldn't be humans— we'd be brainless puppets. And I like my brain. Don't you like yours?"

"I guess." Will shrugged and looked down at his feet while he thought for a moment.

"Look, even if these dogs stay here, Satan will just find another time to tempt Adam and Eve. He watched them and waited for them to mess up. We're humans; we mess up all the time. Satan has plenty of chances to tempt us."

"We have a chance to stop this," Will said, still feeling uncertain about this mission. "What if God wants us to make it right again? We can live happily like Adam and Eve, just picking berries in a world without sin."

Molly narrowed her eyes at Will and shook her head. "God sent us here to correct the story. It's not our place to decide what happens in history. We have to set the story right."

Will shook his head. "No, don't you see? It's our chance to go back to Eden!" He spoke quickly and with great excitement, which made Molly nervous.

"Will, you are doubting yourself. You're doubting us, and you're doubting God's message to us."

"But what if this is the right message?" Will asked, turning around to take in the glory of the garden. "Look at this! This could all be ours! We wouldn't have to suffer anymore! Everything would be good and . . . ."

Whump! Before he could finish his sentence, a huge net fell over him, trapping him. He struggled to get out, but his arms were pinned. He flailed

around, turning to see who or what had
trapped him.

It was Molly.

She glared at him with her hands on her hips. "Listen here, William. I am here to make this Bible story right. Either you can help me, or I can leave you here, but you are not going to talk me into taking another bite of forbidden fruit. That already happened once, and I am going to follow God's will this time. God was smart enough to make this entire universe, so I'm pretty sure He knows what He's doing, even if our human-sized brains can't figure it out."

Will looked at her, stunned. He suddenly realized what he had been saying. "Molly. . .I. . .er. . ." he stammered. He was so ashamed. "I'm so sorry," he whispered, and sat down on the ground.

Molly reached over to pull off the net, but she stopped and raised an eyebrow at him. "Are you going to behave?" she asked.

Will nodded.

Molly yanked the netting off her friend. "Angie said this would be a hard one. I didn't think anything could be harder than fighting off a crocodile, but I guess fighting off sin is pretty tough, too."

"I don't know what happened. It all made so much sense to me that I was convinced I was right. I could have messed up everything—the whole Bible," Will said sadly.

"But you didn't."

"Thanks to you. What if you hadn't been here? I would have ruined everything!"

"But that's why God gave us each other, to build strength. Remember last week's verse? 'Two people are better than one. They can help each other in everything they do.' God gave us each other so we could work together to fight evil. You can't do it on your own." She reached out her hand to pull him up.

"Thanks for being such a good friend," Will said as she helped him stand. "Come on, we have to go save that puppy before its parents get back!"

9

THE RESCUE

They ran back to the tree where the small puppy clung to a branch. It whined and shook with fear.

Molly held out the net and Will took the other side. They stretched it out beneath the branch where the puppy huddled.

"Come on, puppy!" Molly called. "Jump down! We'll catch you!"

The puppy's tail wagged, but it hugged the branch.

Will whistled and clucked for the dog. "Food!" he said, thinking about his dog at home and how it would do anything for a treat. "We need a treat!"

"Berries!" Molly said. Just then, she heard a loud bark across the river and saw two large dogs coming out of the woods. "Quick, its parents are returning!"

Will looked over his shoulder. With a surge of courage, he said to Molly, "Stay here. I'll go get the berries!"

He took off running toward a group of bushes by the water's edge just as the dogs reached the river on the other side.

He swiped a handful of berries and sprinted back to Molly. He could hear the dogs splashing through the water.

He threw the berries on the net and

held one up in the air. "Come on, puppy! Here is a yummy treat!" he said, waving it so the puppy could catch its scent.

The puppy's nose wriggled, its tail wagged, and it reached out to try to bite the fruit, but instead toppled off the branch.

"Catch it!" Molly called as she positioned the net below.

Whoosh! The puppy landed safely, right in the middle of the net.

"Slam dunk!" Will laughed. "My basketball coach would be proud!"

A deep growl made the hairs on Will's neck stand up. He turned around to see the two large dogs surrounding them. They were growling and baring their teeth.

"Look out!" Molly screamed as the dogs lunged at them.

Suddenly a bright light flashed before them.

10

A NEW PET

When the light faded, Will and Molly opened their eyes and blinked. They were back in the basement of St. John's.

"We're okay!" Molly said.

Will checked himself out. "We didn't get eaten by the dogs!"

Just then, they heard something growling behind them. Their eyes grew large with fear as they turned to look.

The small puppy was behind them, its hair bristling with fear. Though it was growling at them, it was so little and cute that Molly and Will could only laugh.

Molly gently picked up the puppy and stroked it to calm it down. "Poor thing is so scared. Time travel is pretty confusing."

"How did it come back with us?" Will asked, reaching over to stroke its fur. The puppy licked them and wagged its tail.

"I see you rescued our puppy," Angie said, stepping around the corner.

"Is it going to be okay?" Molly asked. "We didn't mean to bring it back with us."

"God has a plan for everything," Angie answered, just as the door to Room 3C opened. Molly and Will jumped in surprise, accidentally letting go of the puppy.

Mr. Habersham walked in. "Why are you kids still here?" He stopped short and frowned when he saw the puppy. "What is this?" he asked as the puppy ran over and started licking his shoes.

Will reached out to grab it, but Mr. Habersham picked it up first.

"Sorry," Will said. "It just followed us down here, I'll take it back outside right away."

Mr. Habersham looked at the puppy as it wriggled to free itself from his grip. Suddenly a smile spread across his face. "Nah, that's okay. He's kinda cute."

Will and Molly looked at each other. "Cute?" Molly asked. She had never heard Mr. Habersham use that word.

"Yeah, I've been looking for a dog like this to help keep the mice away."

"You mean, you're going to keep him?" Molly asked.

His smile vanished as he looked at Molly and Will. "You have a problem with that?"

Molly put up her hands and shook her head, "No, not at all," she stammered.

"We should get back to Children's Chapel," Will said, pulling her by the elbow. "There really is a plan for everything," he muttered as they quickly escaped out the door and back into the catacombs.

Genesis 2 - 3 NRSV

Thus the heavens and the earth were finished, and all their multitude. And on the seventh day God finished the work that he had done, and he rested on the seventh day from all the work that he had done. So God blessed the seventh day and hallowed it, because on it God rested from all the work that he had done in creation.

These are the generations of the heavens and the earth when they were created. In the day that the Lord God made the earth and the heavens, when no plant of the field was yet in the earth and no herb of the field had yet sprung up—for the Lord God had not caused it to rain upon the earth, and there was no one to till the ground; but a stream would rise from the earth, and water the whole face of the ground— then the Lord God formed man from the dust of the ground, and breathed into his nostrils the breath of life; and the man became a living being. And the Lord God planted a garden in Eden, in the east; and there he put the man whom he had formed. Out of the ground the Lord God made to grow every tree that is pleasant to the sight and good for food, the tree of life also in the midst of the garden, and the tree of the knowledge of good and evil.

A river flows out of Eden to water the garden, and from there it divides and becomes four branches. The name of the first is Pishon; it is the one that flows around the whole land of Havilah, where there is gold; and the gold of that land is good; bdellium and onyx stone are there. The name of the second river is Gihon; it is the one that flows around the whole land of Cush.

The name of the third river is Tigris, which flows east of Assyria. And the fourth river is the Euphrates.

The Lord God took the man and put him in the garden of Eden to till it and keep it. And the Lord God commanded the man, 'You may freely eat of every tree of the garden; but of the tree of the knowledge of good and evil you shall not eat, for in the day that you eat of it you shall die.' Then the Lord God said, 'It is not good that the man should be alone; I will make him a helper as his partner.' So out of the ground the Lord God formed every animal of the field and every bird of the air, and brought them to the man to see what he would call them; and whatever the man called each living creature, that was its name. The man gave names to all cattle, and to the birds of the air, and to every animal of the field; but for the man there was not found a helper as his partner. So the Lord God caused a deep sleep to fall upon the man, and he slept; then he took one of his ribs and closed up its place with flesh. And the rib that the Lord God had taken from the man he made into a woman and brought her to the man.

Then the man said, 'This at last is bone of my bones and

flesh of my flesh; this one shall be called Woman, for out

of Man this one was taken.' Therefore a man leaves his father and his mother and clings to his wife, and they become one flesh. And the man and his wife were both naked, and were not ashamed. Now the serpent was more crafty than any other wild animal that the Lord God had made. He said to the woman, 'Did God say, "You shall not eat from any tree in the garden"?' The woman said to the serpent, 'We may eat of the fruit of the trees in the garden; but God said, "You shall not eat of the fruit of the tree that is in the middle of the garden, nor shall you touch it, or you shall die." ' But the serpent said to the woman, 'You will not die; for God knows that when you eat of it your eyes will be opened, and you will be like God, knowing good and evil.'

So when the woman saw that the tree was good for food, and that it was a delight to the eyes, and that the tree was to be desired to make one wise, she took of its fruit and ate; and she also gave some to her husband, who was with her, and he ate. Then the eyes of both were opened, and they knew that they were naked; and they sewed fig leaves together and made loincloths for themselves.

They heard the sound of the Lord God walking in the garden at the time of the evening breeze, and the man and his wife hid themselves from the presence of the Lord God among the trees of the garden. But the Lord God called to the man, and said to him, 'Where are you?' He said, 'I heard the sound of you in the garden, and I was afraid, because I was naked; and I hid myself.' He said, 'Who told you that you were naked? Have you eaten from the tree of which I commanded you not to eat?' The man said, 'The woman whom you gave to be with me, she gave me fruit from the tree, and I ate.' Then the Lord God said to the woman, 'What is this that you have done?' The woman said, 'The serpent tricked me, and I ate.' The Lord God said to the serpent, 'Because you have done this, cursed are you among all animalsand among all wild creatures; upon your belly you shall go, and dust you shall eatall the days of your life. I will put enmity between you and the woman, and between your offspring and hers; he will strike your head, and you will strike his heel.' To the woman he said,'I will greatly increase your pangs in childbearing; in pain you shall bring forth children, yet your desire shall be for your husband, and he shall rule over you.' And to the man he said,'Because you have listened to the voice of your wife, and have eaten of the tree about which I commanded you, "You shall not eat of it", cursed is the ground because of you; in toil you shall eat of it

all the days of your life; thorns and thistles it shall bring
forth for you; and you shall eat the plants of the field. By the
sweat of your face you shall eat bread until you return to the
ground for out of it you were taken; you are dust, and to dust
you shall return.'

The man named his wife Eve, because she was the mother of
all who live. And the Lord God made garments of skins for
the man and for his wife, and clothed them.

Then the Lord God said, 'See, the man has become like one
of us, knowing good and evil; and now, he might reach out
his hand and take also from the tree of life, and eat, and live
for ever'— therefore the Lord God sent him forth from the
garden of Eden, to till the ground from which he was taken.
He drove out the man; and at the east of the garden of Eden
he placed the cherubim, and a sword flaming and turning to
guard the way to the tree of life.

ACKNOWLEDGMENTS

Thank you to my fabulous family members and friends who continue to encourage and support my writing. Thank you to all of the local businesses and friends who continue to promote this series. Thank you to the great readers who get so excited to read about the next Will and Molly adventure. Finally, thank you to my dear editor Amie for her great eye.

DON'T MISS WILL AND MOLLY'S OTHER
CATACOMBS MYSTERIES©
ADVENTURES!

#1 Secret of the Catacombs

#2 The Vanishing Act

#3 The Beginning of the End

To learn more about The Catacombs Mysteries©
series and order your next book, visit the author's web
site:

www.MaryLitton.com

ABOUT THE AUTHOR

© Joylyn Hannahs

Mary Litton has lived in the DC area for over 12 years. When she was a girl, her goal was to be a published author by the age of ten. Even though it took a little longer than she expected, she thinks the Catacombs Mysteries© series was worth the wait! She is happily married and the proud mom of two children and one chocolate lab.